THE INVISIBLE GODDESS

A MYTHOLOGICAL RETELLING

A. C. DAWN

CONTENTS

PROLOGUE

I was there when the world began. I was born of chaos and became darkness. Together with the night, I brought forth day and light- opposites to balance the universe. I anchor the day to the night.

What is my name? An eternity has passed since it was spoken. I am unwelcome—and feared. Banished to corners. Pushed aside. I churn in the abyss, forgotten and alone, while the world embraces the light. I am darkness. I am limitless. I am forever.

They were born of boundless power, these infantile gods. They play on Olympus like mortal children playing in the dirt, squandering their abilities in petty games and intrigues. We created a world and wielded the power of the void. What have they done?

I wonder what will become of them...

ONE

"You puffed up peacock. I am the Goddess of Marriage. How do you think it looks when you disregard the very thing I stand for?" Hera hissed with her hands on her hips.

Zeus rolled his eyes at her dramatic accusation. This old argument wearied him.

"You are the Queen of Heaven and first among my wives and all goddesses. What do you care how anything looks? I grow tired of fighting with you, Wife. Why can't you be more like Hestia? See how sweetly she stands, waiting for my command." He beckoned to Hestia, who hurried forward from where she stopped inside the door.

Hestia wasn't waiting for Zeus's command. She wanted to speak to him about her plans for the west garden, but stumbled into one of his endless squabbles with his wife. She'd hesitated a moment too long to make her escape.

"Hestia isn't married to a philanderer. In fact, I think she is the wisest among all of us, abstaining from any romantic entanglements. At least you aren't panting around the hem of her gown like you do that cow, Io." Hera's eyes flashed at the mention of Zeus's latest consort.

A low rumble of thunder echoed around them as Zeus's temper flared. Hestia knew where this was heading. Maybe she could head it off before it got started.

"Dionysus has brought a new vintage for you to try. He says that the grapes were among his sweetest ever. Would you like it served tonight with the fish, or shall we wait and try it with the chicken tomorrow?" Hestia crossed her fingers and caught Zeus's appreciative look from the corner of her eye.

As she predicted, the question about the menu diverted Hera's attention. Though she was the Queen of Heaven and Mistress of Olympus, Hera didn't manage the day to day operations of the court. Hestia saw to the meals, the assemblies, and the constant stream of guests. Hera left it to her but took the credit. She only had an opinion in Zeus's company.

"Silly, Hestia. Why would we wait? Serve it with the fish tonight and make tomorrow's supper pork. We have had far too much chicken lately." Hera issued her orders, and Hestia simply nodded. It didn't matter to her what they served.

Taking advantage of the distraction, Zeus made an excuse and fled before Hera could resume their argument. Hestia didn't wait for Hera to find something else to add to her to-do list. She left the Queen of Heaven standing alone and slipped out the side entrance to the portico.

Hestia pulled in a breath of the sweet clean air that was unique to the mountain. Perfumed by waves of ever-blooming flowers and stirred by gentle breezes, Mount Olympus was a paradise and the only home she had ever known. For as long as she could remember, she filled her days running the court, seeing to everyone's comfort, and anticipating their needs. Usually, she enjoyed it, but lately her spirit felt restless, caged, and resentful.

With a sigh, she wandered to the far end of the palace. She didn't worry about changing the plans in the kitchen. Hera would forget all about her instructions by dinner. She should speak to Katrina, her head paige, to confirm the preparation of Demeter's chambers. The Goddess of the Harvest was due to return any day from her inspection of the crops. There were other things Hestia ought to do, but she couldn't find any enthusiasm for them.

As she reached the southern boundary of the palace gardens, movement in the corner caught her eye. She grinned and sat down on the bench next to the path.

"Is that the King of Gods lurking behind a fig tree?" she asked, looking over the gardens and away from where Zeus tried ineffectually to conceal himself.

A rueful smile tugged at his lips as he joined her on the bench. "I don't lurk. I was inspecting the figs."

"You were hiding from your wife," Hestia replied with a laugh.

"Well, that too. I thought Hera might have followed you." Zeus paused as he picked a nearby bloom and twirled it between his fingers. Trying to sound nonchalant, he announced, "Io and the priestesses from Argo will arrive today. Put them in the eastern chambers."

Hestia closed her eyes for a moment. Io's arrival would enrage Hera, even though Io was one of her priestesses. There would be no peace on Olympus today. Hestia suddenly felt weary to the core. She stood and left Zeus on the bench. He could deal with his own intrigues.

"Hestia," Zeus called after. "I expect you to see to it."

His voice held a rumble of displeasure that he typically reserved for misbehaving gods.

Hestia kept walking. The chambers were ready. They were always ready, but Zeus would never notice that. Just as he never noticed her unless he wanted something. She wasn't like the other goddesses with their flashy beauty and vain obsessions. She thrived in the peace and tranquility of a well-ordered house. Her appearance was only important insofar that she, too, should be neat and tidy.

The garden gave way to a little footpath that led to the mountain's highest peak. Hestia followed it mindlessly. Discontent gnawed at her, and having never experienced it before, she didn't know what to do with it. The palace felt cramped. She never had a moment to herself and wondered why that bothered her. Her joy came from seeing to the needs of others.

Hestia ran her fingers through the needles of a black fir tree that struggled to find purchase between two boulders. She had sympathy for the plant that struggled to grow, squeezed between two giants that wouldn't give an inch. She pulled a few needles off and inhaled the refreshing pine scent. The tree didn't care about the boulders squashing it. It grew and flourished despite them. Hestia turned her face to the sun and tried to absorb the tree's lesson.

The rocky path grew steeper, but she pressed on, choosing her path carefully in the loose rock. Puffing slightly from the climb, she sat on one of the boulders that littered the summit and took in the breathtaking vista.

TWO

Her soul settled a bit as she shook off the uncharacteristic melancholy. Hestia looked down on the tops of the clouds and considered lying down among them for a moment. She hadn't done that for ages. She used to run and jump from cloud to cloud, making Zeus laugh. Those were the days when the world was new, and they had been young and full of innocence-- some more innocent than others.

At the edge of the cloud line, Hestia noticed a fissure in the sheer rock face. A faint light stirred within it. She'd never seen it before, though she had wandered this path countless times. Intrigued, she pushed to her feet and slipped from her perch. Olympus held many secrets under her skirt.

Wide enough for a mortal man to pass through, the jagged crack was wider than Hestia initially thought. The flickering light beckoned her. She hesitated a moment, but curiosity propelled her forward. An enormous cavern opened before her. The light seemed to be all around, dimly glowing with no discernible source. Shadows layered on shadows.

Hestia stepped forward. Her foot slipped on a sharp edge, and an abyss of darkness opened before her. She windmilled her arms, trying to reverse her momentum. She pitched forward with a scream. A hard gust of a warm wind caught her and pushed her back from the brink. Stumbling, she pressed herself against the cool stone walls and gulped down breaths as her heart hammered in her chest. The eerie glow undulated around her, revealing a narrow ledge that gave way to a bottomless pit.

A coarse laugh echoed around the chamber, though she could see no one. Of course, on Olympus, the birthplace of magic and life, anything was possible.

"Who's there?" she demanded, staying firmly against the wall.

"Are all the Olympians as foolish as you?" The voice sounded hoarse and gravelly, like it hadn't been used in a very long time.

"I don't consider myself a fool. Who are you? Why do you hide in the shadows?"

Hestia edged toward the crevice in the rock. She may be an immortal goddess born of the Titans, but immortality would be a long time to spend at the bottom of a black pit. She could get herself out of an ordinary hole, but it was rapidly becoming clear, there was nothing ordinary about this situation. She had the strongest impression that whoever lurked in the darkness had lured her here, but for what purpose she couldn't fathom. A macabre thought struck her. How long would it take for someone to even notice she was missing?

"Poor Hestia. No one notices you. Did you know they call you the invisible goddess?" the voice taunted.

Hestia winced in the darkness. She often felt invisible, but she thought a well-kept house should seem to run itself.

Another gust of warm air buffeted her. It swirled around her like a tempest, pushing her toward the brink. She flailed wildly. Her fingers brushed the rough surface of the cavern walls without finding purchase, and her feet stepped out onto nothing. Blackness engulfed her as she fell. Terror rose in her throat as she braced herself for the bottom, but it never came.

"Are you a goddess? Do you not wield the power of Olympus?" The voice echoed in her mind, lazily goading her. "Will you not save yourself, Hestia? Perhaps you are no better than a common human, after all."

Air rushed past Hestia. She twisted and tumbled in the darkness. Anger flared hot at the words. Her unseen tormenter would answer for his insults. With a thought, she stopped falling. Channeling her powers, she flooded the cave with fire and, in a blink, was standing back on the precipice.

Furious with herself as much as with her tormenter, she took a deep breath as fire danced around her. Hestia rarely used the flames that were at her command. Mild-mannered and quiet, she used her fire to warm and comfort- never for destruction or aggression. But as she stood with long-forgotten power coursing through her, she wondered if she had let herself fade too much to the background. Heady power filled her as the long-denied heat burned in her belly. It felt good.

Hestia looked down into the endless void, where even her divine light could not penetrate. Erebus, the primordial god of darkness, churned in his bodiless state, cringing away from the brightness. Though eons had passed since Erebus' time, she knew him instantly. Like many of the primordial gods, he was a relic, forgotten in favor of the next generation of gods. He helped shape the world, but in recent times, their forefathers had largely retired out of sight and out of mind. Why he had showed himself to her, she didn't know, but a millennium of lying dormant in the bowels of the earth had done nothing to improve his disposition.

"What would you know of it, King of Darkness and consort of night? You fill the cracks and crevices of the world—shapeless, nameless, forgotten. You have no right to point fingers at me, dark one. Hide your face in the shadows and leave me alone."

Hestia whirled around and ran out of the cavern. She left the fires burning behind her.

Erebus's shouts and curses chased her down the path. The light would dim over time, but perhaps it would make the crotchety old god think twice before he meddled in the affairs of Olympus. Still, Hestia suffered a pang of regret at her sharp words. What had gotten into her today? She would return to the cave tomorrow and apologize to Erebus. At the moment, she needed to get ready for the evening meal. She hurried back toward the palace.

Thunder rumbled, and lightning flashed across the sky. Hestia could hear Hera's displeased shouts as she reached the edge of the garden. She shook her head and resigned herself to play peacemaker once again. Maybe old Erebus was right. She had been silent for long enough. A boldness came over her, making her almost giddy as she swept into the assembly hall where Hera and Zeus hurled insults at each other.

"Be silent! Both of you hold your barbed tongues!" Hestia came to a stop between the bickering pair, who both fell silent at her unprecedented interruption. "Zeus, we all know better than attempt to curtail your affairs, but do not bring them to the palace as a direct insult to your queen."

Hera drew a breath to launch into another diatribe, but Hestia put up her hand to quell the outburst. Sparks leapt from her fingertips, surprising her as much as Zeus, whose eyes went wide at the display of temper.

"Hera, quit your harping! It won't change him. He always comes back to you in the end. Be content." Hestia paused and looked back and forth between the dumbstruck couple. No one dared to challenge them, but coming from meek and mild Hestia, it was doubly unfathomable. "You have upset the tranquility of this house, and as goddess of the home, I will not have it. Now, I suggest both of you collect yourselves so you can behave like civilized gods at the evening meal."

Hestia exited the same way she came in and checked on the preparations for dinner. Everything was ready, as it should be. Her body hummed with energy and purpose. Charged with excitement, she dressed for dinner. On impulse, she left her customary veil on the dressing table and lined her eyes with charcoal. She wove golden ribbon through her red hair and draped a heavy golden torque around her neck. Smiling, she left her chamber and immediately ran into Zeus.

"Sister, do not challenge me like that again," he rumbled, but stopped short, taking in her appearance. "You look lovely. You should dress like that more often. I enjoy seeing your face." He turned and offered his arm. She slipped her hand in the crook of his elbow as he headed for the great hall. "I will host a celebration in Hera's honor in three days. You'll take care of it?" He looked down at her and grinned.

Hestia didn't answer. The shadows thrown by the

lamps caught her eye. She had the strangest impression that the shadows were moving with them. Was that shadow darker than it should be? She squinted at the offending dark spot, and her feet came to a halt.

"Hestia? Did you hear me," Zeus demanded and stopped to look down at her before turning his gaze to follow hers. "What is it?"

Hestia shook herself. She was being foolish. "It's nothing. Just something caught my eye. Of course, Zeus, I'll take care of everything," Hestia replied, squeezing his arm in reassurance.

An unexpected thrill of anticipation ran through her. Usually, a celebration meant planning and preparation. For the first time, her mind went to dancing instead of menus and music. Maybe there could be more to her life than linens and guest lists. Maybe it was time for her to move out of the shadows.

～

No one ever noticed my cave before, but she found me. She burned me. For so long, I've felt nothing, as empty as the void. She was strong, the Goddess of Flame, and she knew me. She understands so much more than her siblings. Her fire is pure, untainted with avarice and power, but so many other shining ones overshadow it.

These Olympians are poor replacements for the mighty Titans. How they ever prevailed, I don't know. They have squandered their victory. They populated the earth and retired to their mountain to bicker and quarrel with each other. They disgust me.

But this one, the Goddess of Hearth and Home. She is different. She deserves to be seen, to be revered. In their *homes, the mortals honor her first before any other, but her fellow gods forget she even exists. That must change, but she will not do it herself. She needs a partner to lead her into the light.*

Who is worthy of her? Zeus? That philanderer has too many goddesses already. Hades has power aplenty, but he would hide her away in the world below. What of Poseidon, the Earth Shaker and God of the Sea? Yes, he has power and room for a wife.

What about the younger gods? Hephaestus- the cripple? No. The poor fool has his hands full with Aphrodite. Hermes, son of Zeus, enjoys playing games and making mischief far too much. Zeus has another son, Apollo. Strong, passionate, and a poet. Perhaps he will do.

Would the Goddess of Flame want passion or power? Which will it be? The Earth Shaker or the Archer Prince. Who will win Hestia's hand?

THREE

"Welcome, Aphrodite. You look lovely," Hestia said with a smile as the Goddess of Love walked into the assembly hall.

Hestia glanced down at her simple, dowdy gown and suddenly wished she had given into the urge to borrow one of Hera's robes. Aphrodite sparkled with gold ornaments wrapped around her arms and slender neck. They accented her barely-there gown and enhanced the goddess's perfection.

"Of course, I do," Aphrodite quipped without hesitation. "Especially when I'm standing next to that." She hooked her thumb toward her husband, Hephaestus, and with a toss of her golden curls, swept off into the multitude of gods and demigods that swarmed around the room.

Hephaestus said nothing. He was used to his wife's sharp tongue, though Hestia suspected it bothered him more than he let on. He kissed Hestia on the cheek and surveyed the room with a disgusted look.

"Zeus has gone all out. Will this get him back in my mother's good graces?"

Hestia smiled. "He gave her a new necklace. Poseidon brought it from the depths of the sea, and Hera has already forgotten their spat."

"Well, you have been busy, my dear. I know whose hard work put this together."

The God of the Forge squeezed her shoulder gently with one of his powerful hands. Hestia wondered again how Aphrodite could be so blind. Hephaestus could best Ares with one arm behind his back and his crippled legs.

"Enjoy the party, Hestia," he murmured in her ear before he limped toward Dionysus and the freely flowing wine.

Hestia turned to greet the next guest. Apollo stood before her, resplendent in white robes, and utterly gorgeous. Her stomach flipped at the sight of him. His fair hair glinted in the light, and his blue eyes danced with excitement as he looked over the assembly.

"Hestia!"

Apollo caught her up in his arms and swung her around in a circle. Caught off guard, she gasped and clung to him. His muscular body pressed to hers, and for a moment, all she could hear was the pounding of her own heart. He sat her down and smiled at her, but didn't move to put any distance between them.

"You've outdone yourself! The palace looks marvelous." He leaned down and whispered in her ear. "I've been naughty, so I better confess. I stole some sweetmeats from the kitchen. You're not mad, are you?"

He straightened and looked down at Hestia with mock seriousness. He couldn't keep up the façade and grinned. With a flourish, he twirled her in a circle and dipped her deeply. Hestia's head reeled as he pulled her back to her feet. She gripped his shoulders as the room spun around her.

"Be sure to save me a dance later. I have a feeling this is going to be a delightful evening." His words tumbled out enthusiastically as he surveyed the room before turning his eyes back to her. He paused for a moment, as if considering something.

Hestia held her breath, waiting for him to turn her loose. With a quick jerk of his hand, Apollo tugged her veil off and tossed it away. Before Hestia could manage more than a squeak of reproach, he kissed her. Not a friendly kiss of greeting, but a heart-pounding, toe-curling kiss.

She melted against him, her body humming in response. No one had ever kissed her like this. Heat flashed deep within her as Apollo teased her lips apart. Her head spun as she opened her mouth, excited and unsure.

A loud cough from behind them brought Hestia back to her senses. She pushed away from the Archer Prince and hastily straightened her gown.

"Enjoy the party, Apollo," she choked out as she turned to face Poseidon. His mouth pressed in a firm line of disapproval. "My Lord of the Sea, welcome! Has Amphitrite joined us on land tonight?" Hestia forced a bright smile while her cheeks blushed crimson.

"My wife has stayed below the waves for the night. What are you doing, letting the poet grope you like that? You're not a serving maid." Poseidon demanded, his face clouding with rage. "Has his silver tongue beguiled you? Have you given yourself to him?"

"What if I had?" Hestia shot back, irritated that he would question her. "I am not a child. You, Zeus, and the rest cavort as you see fit. Why can't I?"

"Because you are the best amongst us," Poseidon

replied, his tone suddenly softer. "You are all that is good and right in this world. I would not have you spoiled."

He raised her hand to his lips and pressed a kiss against her palm. His tousled hair fell over his forehead, and his storm gray eyes locked onto hers. For a moment, they were the only two people in the world. Then a smile split his lips, and he let her hand go. He shook his head as he pushed into the crowd.

Hestia stared after him. Her wits lay scattered in her mind like wheat blown from the shaft. What was going on? Nobody ever said more than a friendly greeting. Ever since the incident in the cave, an odd sense of anticipation gnawed at her, like something exciting was going to happen soon, but she didn't know what it was.

With an effort, Hestia shook off the feeling. She didn't have time for such foolishness. She had a party to run. She nodded at Athena in greeting and went to check on the Muses. They should have been singing by now. Fickle creatures. They were never where they were supposed to be.

FOUR

Hours later, Hestia sat outside on the portico and
listened as the Muses' voices rose in perfect
harmony. She peeked over the ledge of the
window. Garlands of lilies draped either side, flooding the
area with their heady fragrance. She watched the gods and
goddesses ebb and flow as they followed the patterned line
dance. Next would come a partner dance, the Antikristos.
She wondered how they would pair off, knowing that no
one would ask for her hand. With a sigh, she turned away
and leaned back against the cool marble facade of the
palace, losing herself in the lilting rhythm of the music.

Hestia imagined twirling around the dance floor. Her
partner held her close and led them confidently among the
others. She floated along, never tripping or falling out of
time. Elegant and lovely as Aphrodite, Hestia danced in a
flowing gown that clung to her like a second skin. Her curls
fell from their pins and tickled her bare shoulders. Everyone
stopped dancing and watched them.

A harsh cough interrupted her daydream. Hestia
snapped her eyes open and looked around, but she stood

alone on the deserted portico. Shifting in the shadows caught her attention. She looked closer and frowned. In the corner of the green patch of grass, a bench and quietly burbling fountain sat in the evening shade. As she stared, an inky spot detached itself from the shadows below the bench.

Bodiless, Erebus possessed no defined shape. He could grow or shrink at will. As the elemental darkness of the world, he shunned bright, open spaces, preferring corners, caves, and closets. He oozed out from under the bench and spread like a puddle in the shady corner of the portico. Moving slowly, he crept up the cool sheen of the marble wall and shaped himself to mimic Hestia's posture, like a malignant shadow.

Hestia put her hands on her hips, and Erebus matched her movement. She rolled her eyes and glared at him, in no mood for his taunting. The long, confusing evening left her weary, and she longed for the quiet solitude of her rooms.

"What's brought slinking out of your pit? I thought you didn't like the light."

"It's not so light now," the grating voice answered. "Night is falling. It is the time for shadows. How is your party? Why are you out here alone and not dancing? Will no one dance with you?" Erebus drew out his questions in long, languid syllables that dripped with insincere concern.

"I was just taking a break from all the dancing. I needed some air," Hestia retorted.

"Liar." The word, laced with venom, echoed across the deserted portico.

The shadow on the wall expanded, morphing into a towering menace that stretched over her head and across the ceiling.

Hestia felt cold and small. Under the immensity of the

shadow, her desires rose in sharp relief. She told herself she didn't have time for dancing. A hostess had too many other duties to manage, but as the darkness so bluntly put it, she was a liar. In all the countless years and all the countless dances, no one had ever asked her to dance.

Tears pricked at her eyes, and she ground her teeth together in frustration. She had never been unhappy with her lot before. She was the most content of the goddesses, happy as long as she had a house to keep. What had awakened these desires? She wished they had stayed hidden, dormant, and forgotten. She wanted her old comfort, not this constant hope that something--anything--might happen.

Erebus laughed like stone grating against stone. "I've never seen a more pitiful sight- a goddess feeling sorry for herself. You're a disgrace to your heritage, but I want to help you."

Hestia snapped out of her downward spiral. Of course, Erebus was responsible for her unrest. He sowed discord like the mortals sowed wheat in their fields.

"I neither need nor want your help. Go back to your hole and rot. No one will notice you've gone." She whirled around, intending to rejoin the party.

"Not quite yet," Erebus whispered.

In a blink, he surrounded her. Hestia's heart galloped in momentary panic as impenetrable darkness clamped around her. It evaporated as quickly as it had come, stealing her balance, and leaving her reeling.

Hestia's arms groped for something to steady her as her eyes adjusted to the sudden brightness. Apollo was there, reaching out to offer his support. She grabbed ahold gratefully and didn't resist when he stepped closer to pull her against him.

"Are you alright, Hestia? I've been looking for you all

evening. How am I to dance with you if you're out here on the portico?" Apollo's silky smooth voice soothed her, and for a moment, she didn't even notice what he had said.

"Dance with you?" Hestia hadn't meant to sound like a stunned parrot, but no one had ever asked her to dance. She had to stop this foolishness. "I don't dance, Apollo." She pulled away from him, but his arm around her waist tightened its hold. "I have much to see to." Undeterred, he caught her hand and pinned it against his chest. His body pressed against hers. Doggedly, she tried one more time, "You'll need to let me go if you expect the sweetmeats to be presented on time." She pushed at his arm, but it yielded as much as the marble wall.

"Listen." Apollo murmured against her ear, sending delicious shivers down her spine.

A slow, lyrical melody drifted through the window. One of the Muses, Melpomene, if Hestia wasn't mistaken, began a haunting song about a maiden who had lost her only love. The Muse of Tragedy spun the melody, drawing out each note to perfection. Hestia's heart ached for the maiden, and the music held her spellbound.

Apollo whispered, as if he didn't want to break the spell. "They've started the Antikristos. Give me this one dance. I cannot let the night end without a dance with the most beautiful goddess on Olympus. I've always admired you, Hestia."

A thrill ran through her, and she gasped as he suddenly straightened. Before she could protest, Apollos spun them expertly in a circle.

Hestia had no words as she lifted her gaze to meet his. His sharp crystal blue eyes held the smokiness of desire as he moved them into the dance. She tried to follow, but pitched forward, off-balance. Her feet felt rooted to the ground. She glanced down to see a pool of shadow under them, and with an ungoddess-like growl, she stamped her foot sharply against the marble tile.

"What is it?" Apollo asked, looking at their feet.

The shadow dissolved, but the magic of the moment slipped away. Hestia smiled up at the Archer Prince, unsure of how to feel. Erebus slithered back to a shadowy corner. Relief vied with anger at his interference. He likely saved her from making a fool of herself, but the meddlesome creature should mind his own affairs.

"Just a bug," Hestia said with a shrug of her shoulder. "I really should get back to the kitchens, Apollo."

She twisted in his embrace, but the God of Poetry was not that easily deterred. He pulled her against him, holding her from behind. His golden curls brushed her cheek as he pressed a kiss to her neck that sent shivers of pleasure through her. His arms snaked around her waist, and he tucked a small golden scroll in the belt of her gown. The heat of him made Hestia gasp. Her eyes drifted closed, and she held her breath, wishing she had the power to suspend time.

"I believe all that nonsense you spew has rotted your ears. Hestia told you to let her go." Poseidon's deep voice carried over the soft music as he emerged from the assembly hall. His dark storm-swept hair fell over his shoulders, and his mouth drew down in a disapproving frown.

Apollo made no move to release her. He swayed gently back and forth in time with the music. "I thought I smelled fish. Hestia and I are dancing. Go away."

Hestia rolled her eyes. This was ridiculous. Roughly, she pushed Apollo's arms away from her. He let them drop unresisting, but before she could say anything, Apollo brushed a kiss across her lips. He slipped his fingers under her chin and tipped her head back until her gaze met his. His thumb ran over her lower lip and desire rolled through her as his eyes promised so many other pleasures she only vaguely understood, but longed to know more about.

"Another time. Read the scroll and give me your answer," he murmured.

Without another word to Poseidon, Apollo disappeared into the great hall.

FIVE

The small scroll felt as heavy as a stone, but Hestia forced herself not to pull it out and read it immediately. Giddiness and excitement surged through her. Apollo, the silver-tongued poet, unequaled archer, and soldier, thought her beautiful, told her he admired her, and asked her to dance. Even as inexperienced as Hestia was with matters of love and lust, she could read the desire in Apollo's eyes.

Poseidon interrupted her thoughts.

"To the depths with that golden-haired pretty boy. You've had a long day. Let's sit and talk for a while. I know the kitchens can do without you for a bit longer." Poseidon offered her his arm.

Hestia stared at him, unsure of what to do. Poseidon intimidated her, and she usually tried to avoid him. She thought him a brute and a bully. He threw tantrums that destroyed cities and took whatever woman he wanted—willing or not. But he had never looked at her the way he was looking at her now. Those storm-tossed gray eyes looked at her with tenderness and appreciation. Weariness tugged at her, but she knew it wasn't from her duties of the day.

Confused and curious, Hestia took Poseidon's arm and let him lead her to the bench by the fountain. The water burbled happily, and they sat together in companionable silence, watching the water flow. Hestia sighed, relaxed by the quiet serenity.

The God of the Sea flicked his fingers at the fountain. The water shaped into dolphins that jumped and splashed. Then, a mighty whale rose up and breached in the pool, followed by a sea turtle. Hestia laughed in delight. He entertained her with all manner of sea creatures, many of which she had never even heard of.

"The sea is full of marvels," Poseidon told her.

"I never imagined. I always thought it was cold and dark and wet." Hestia blushed at the foolishness of her statement, but Poseidon chuckled.

"You get used to the wet." Poseidon tucked one of Hestia's coppery curls behind her ear. He shifted his position, leaning closer to her. Hestia's stomach flipped. First, Apollo had made her head spin, and now Poseidon made her heart melt with his gentleness. "The poet had one thing right. You are the most beautiful goddess on Olympus."

Hestia didn't know what to say. She looked at the fountain that was once again a fountain and sighed. Overwhelmed by the night's event, she couldn't think of a response. Poseidon gave her a sympathetic smile. Without another word, he wrapped his arms around her and cradled her against him. Awash in the tenderness of his embrace, she leaned into him. Poseidon brushed his hand up and down her back. Contentment and warmth washed over her.

"I could have a wife on land and in the sea. Would you do me the honor of being my wife, Hestia? You would have a home of your own and wouldn't have to deal with Zeus and Hera anymore. Any man, god or mortal, would be proud to be your husband."

Hestia jerked away and stared at the God of the Sea. He still wore his tender, affectionate expression and was utterly and stupefyingly serious. Her brows knitted together, and she brought her hands up in an ineffectual gesture to erase Poseidon's words. Where had that come from? Before today, Poseidon had never given her a second glance. She opened her mouth and snapped it closed again when nothing would come out.

The grating laughter of Erebus echoed around them. Poseidon looked around, startled, but before Hestia could say anything, the bench they sat on bucked violently, dumping them both on the ground. Hestia saw the dark, slithering shadow of Erebus as he disappeared into the falling night.

Poseidon jumped to his feet and whirled around, searching for his enemy and cursing foully. Hestia seized the moment. She scrambled to her feet and ran. Without breaking stride, she pelted around the side entrance and through the kitchen, ignoring Katrina's calls. Her sandals slapped against the marble tiles, sending echoes through the empty halls. She skidded to a stop at the entrance to her chambers and slipped inside, closing the door firmly behind her. Leaning against the door, she gulped down breaths as her heart hammered in her chest.

The world had gone mad. Her stomach flipped all over again when she thought about the tender touch of Poseidon's hand and the look in his stormy eyes when he asked for her hand. The tantalizing prospect of having her own house free of the court and all its demands danced in her mind.

She collapsed face first on her bed with a groan. It was all too much to think about. Apollo's scroll dug into her belly. She'd forgotten it. With a fresh surge of excitement, she rolled over and yanked the scroll from her belt.

Hair of flame

Heart of gold

Loyal, true, and beloved by all who know you

Beloved by me

I treasure your purity

And long to feel the burn of your fire

Marry me, Hestia, and let us live and love for eternity

Hestia let the scroll drop from her hands and stared at the canopy above her bed. How had the world gone so topsy-turvy in a few short days? Excitement vied with fear and uncertainty as she turned the night's events over in her mind.

Two marriage proposals and a primordial god bent on meddling in her life. What she would give to be plain old Hestia again. Even as the thought crossed her mind, she knew it for a lie. The last several days held more experiences and emotions than years upon years of her past—and she liked it.

Hestia couldn't go back to the ball and face Poseidon and Apollo again. She called Katrina to her and gave instructions for the rest of the night. In the solitude of chambers, she took off her simple gown and hung it neatly on a peg. On impulse, she stood before her polished silver mirror. She studied her reflection, wondering what Apollo and Poseidon suddenly saw so differently. To her eyes, she looked the same as always. She blew out a long sigh, slipped her nightdress over her head, and slipped into bed, where she tried vainly not to think.

Hours later she kicked off the twisted sheets and swung

her legs over the side of the bed. Her mind would not yield to the weariness of her body. Maybe a walk would help.

The dancing had stopped for the night, and quiet darkness engulfed the palace. Wary of running into Erebus, Hestia conjured a light in her hand and illuminated the path to the garden. Along the row of ever blooming roses, movement caught her eye. She spun toward it. The light dancing on her palm flared and revealed the King of the Gods slinking through the night.

Zeus called out in surprise. "Sister! What are you doing in the garden this time of night?" he demanded as he came out of the shadows and frowned down at her.

"I could ask the same of you, Zeus, but it's no secret what you are doing. Are you sneaking to or from Io's chambers?"

Zeus's brows lifted at her acid tone. "What has gotten into you, Hestia? Where did you disappear to tonight? Everyone was looking for you."

Hestia scoffed. "Everyone was looking for me?"

"Well, mainly Poseidon and Apollo," Zeus replied. He fell silent for a moment and scratched his chin. He watched her carefully as he continued. "They both asked for your hand in marriage. I confess I didn't know you had a desire to wed."

The blood drained from Hestia's face, and the light sputtered in her palm. She closed her fist, extinguishing it, and let her hand fall to her side.

She found her voice. "I don't. I mean, I didn't before tonight. I," she stumbled over the words as her stomach pitched like a boat on stormy seas. "I just don't know." She trailed off and stared into the darkness, unsure what to think.

Tis going well, this plan. With hardly a whisper in their ear, the Archer and the Earth Shaker were quick enough to come around. Why wouldn't they? Beautiful, strong, and true. Goddess of Fire, Mistress of Flame. How could they have overlooked her before? She is as bright as I am dark.

She flinches away from me. Why shouldn't she? Dark one. Consort of night. Anger, strife, hate... These are what darkness means. It wasn't always. Once, darkness meant peace and stillness. It was the pause before the light. Once, I was welcome. Once, I was worshipped. But not now.

The world fears the Darkness.

SIX

"For the Goddess of Hearth and Home, she sure sleeps late. Shouldn't she be up overseeing the kitchens and the staff?" Aphrodite complained. "It's not like she needs beauty sleep. No amount of sleep will help her be as beautiful as me."

Hera scoffed. "As if your beauty is worth envying."

"She's not asleep," Athena cut in before a fight could erupt. "She's been awake for several minutes, apparently hoping we'll go away."

"How do you know?" Aphrodite asked, and poked Hestia's leg through the bedcovers.

"Her breathing changed, and she opened her eyes for a peek at least three times," Athena replied. As the Goddess of War, she noticed every nuance around her, always on high alert. "Come now, Sister. Wake up and face the day. We'll not leave until you do."

Hestia scrunched her eyes shut and pulled the covers over her head. She'd been awake when the three goddesses marched into her room just after dawn. Zeus must have told them of last night's events. Now they wanted to hear all the gossip for themselves. Aphrodite snatched the covers away, and Hestia shivered as the cool air washed over her warm body. She sat up and pulled her knees up to her chest, glaring at Aphrodite.

The Goddess of Love sprawled lazily at the foot of Hestia's bed while Hera curled like a cat in a chair. Athena stood staring out the window, looking bored and twirling a dagger in hand.

"You three are worse than washerwomen at the well, gossiping and gabbing," Hestia snapped.

"Have you decided?" Hera demanded. "Which one will you wed?"

Hestia closed her eyes and rested her forehead on her knees. Damn Zeus and his big mouth. She tossed and turned much of the night, wrestling with that question.

"I don't know," she mumbled into her knees.

"You must choose Apollo," Hera urged, surprising Hestia. Hera had nothing but contempt for Zeus's illegitimate son. Hestia raised her head and gave Hera a questioning look. "Apollo will love and worship you. He will raise you up in verse, and I dare say in other ways as well." Hera gave her a meaningful look that made Hestia blush crimson.

"Poseidon is the obvious choice." Aphrodite chimed in. "Apollo may write pretty words, but Poseidon commands the seas. He has the power to crush his enemies and bend others to his will. Pretty words and passionate nights are well and good, but why marry a prince when you could have a king?"

Hera shook her head. "Poseidon is more powerful, to be sure. But he will not share that power with you. He'll use it to control you. Take it from one who lives with a tyrant."

Hestia listened to the unsolicited advice and rested her

forehead back on her knees to hide her face as she considered. Poseidon's power was beyond question, but the memory of his tender embrace replayed in her mind. His kind consideration of her comfort and needs warred with his brutal reputation. Besides, she wouldn't be his only wife. He spent much of his time below the sea. He called her the best among them. A rush of pride and affection swept through her as she remembered his praise.

Thoughts of Apollo quickly followed. Hestia tucked the scroll with his beautiful words under her pillow. His breath on her neck and his arms around her ignited heat in her core. He made her want to run wild in the hills and take pleasure in him and only him. He didn't want her to be a homemaker. He wanted her to be a goddess.

Life had gotten very complicated, very quickly. Hestia avoided court intrigues. She always stayed separate, above the clandestine romances and stolen passions. Now, here she was, right in the middle of one. She knew better than to think either Hera or Aphrodite had her best interest at heart.

"I don't think I love either of them," Hestia said after a long pause. She hated to admit how much she liked how they made her feel, but neither Poseidon nor Apollo stirred feelings of love in her heart.

Aphrodite laughed. "Don't be a child, Hestia. Love has nothing to do with it. But," she paused and gave Hestia a calculating look, "If that is important to you, I can make you fall madly, passionately in love with either of them. Which one will it be?"

Hestia's gut clenched. Aphrodite had the power to make Hestia fall blindly in love with a toadstool. In Hestia's opinion, Aphrodite's powers were among the most terrible. By controlling the fickle emotion of love, she could make gods and mortals believe in something that wasn't there. They would give their last breath for it, convinced they were offering themselves up for the noble cause of love. Hestia wanted no part of Aphrodite's magic.

"Aren't you a little cynical for the Goddess of Love?" Hera asked, nettling Aphrodite. "She doesn't need your little magic spell. Choose Apollo, Hestia, and I'll bless your marriage with fertility and happiness."

Aphrodite leaned in toward Hestia and spoke in low tones, though the others could clearly hear every word. "Hera's worried that you'll usurp her if you marry Poseidon. The Earth Shaker might be the second son, but his power is undeniable. Of course, you're well-loved among many, which she cannot claim." Aphrodite's smile turned wicked. "She doesn't want you to come out of the shadows, my dear."

"And you, the mistress of intrigue and guile, have her best interest in mind?" Hera glared at Aphrodite. "You're concerned everyone will think you're losing your touch if you can't play matchmaker."

Hestia groaned and flopped back on the bed. Aphrodite and Hera ignored her, but before they could continue their bickering, Athena spoke.

"You don't have to choose either of them. You can remain untouched and just as you are, Hestia." Athena continued to stare out the window. She had left off her customary greaves and breastplate. Without them, she looked feminine and soft, though Hestia knew she was still as lethal as she was in full armor. Athena broke her gaze away from the world outside and rammed her dagger into its sheath on her belt. She looked at Hestia with a fierce intensity. "Marry or don't marry. Just be sure it's your choice."

The Goddess of War swept from Hestia's chamber, and the

three goddesses were silent for a moment in her wake. Hestia's thoughts tumbled over each other in her mind, creating a jumbled mess that frustrated her. Indecision did not plague her. She didn't worry about love and lust. She made sure they served dinner on time and the guests were comfortable. She blessed the mortals with content homes and healthy, happy communities. These were her passions, but she couldn't deny the strange new feelings awakened in her over the last several days.

Hera and Aphrodite both spoke at once, eager to continue their argument, but a knock on the door interrupted them. Katrina poked her head in, and Hestia could have hugged her in gratitude.

"My Lady, Hestia, the kitchen--," Katrina began.

Hestia catapulted herself off her bed and pulled a wrap around her shoulders.

"Yes, of course! I'll come straight away to the kitchens," she said and hurried out the door, herding a shocked Katrina in front of her.

In the hallway, Katrina finished her sentence. "The kitchens have the morning meal ready. I was wondering if you wanted me to bring you a tray in your room."

Hestia smiled at her friend. "The last place I want to be is my room. Fetch me some clothes, and I will go down to oversee the morning meal."

Katrina hurried away, and Hestia let herself into the small anteroom to the kitchen. She used it as a drying room for herbs. She took a deep breath and tranquility washed over her with the familiar scents of oregano, sage, thyme, and many more. She rolled a sprig of rosemary between her hands and worked the oil through her hair, humming the song of the maiden as she waited for Katrina to bring her gown.

"So, how does it feel to be out of the shadows?"

Hestia jumped and whirled around to find Erebus coiled amongst the shadows of the drying herbs. She frowned at him and pulled her wrap tighter around her.

"What have you done? You, the maker of shadows and master of darkness, have caused all of this turmoil," Hestia accused.

"The Archer and the Earth Shaker only needed a little encouragement. They already desired you. They just needed to notice you." Erebus undulated slowly among the herbs as he answered her in a tone usually reserved for explaining simple concepts to children.

Hestia frowned at him while her mind reeled. Apollo and Poseidon desired her, even before Erebus's interference? Impossible to believe. Before last night, she would have sworn they couldn't even describe her face.

"But, why?" she asked, coming to the heart of what her mind couldn't fathom.

Erebus swelled, oozing out of the nooks and crannies of the herbs, to hang like smoke in the air. The chamber filled with impenetrable darkness. Hestia shivered but made no move to banish the cold blackness. She wanted the answer to her question. After being dormant for eons without as much as a whisper, what had caused Erebus to show himself now? More than that, what had compelled him to take an interest in her?

Erebus laughed his horrible grating laugh. "I told you before I want to help you."

Hestia scoffed and rolled her eyes. She drew breath to argue, but Erebus turned from shadow to substance, pressing against every inch of her and silencing her half-formed words. Her cheeks flamed at the intimacy. She stood frozen like a statue, unwilling to give him the satisfaction of making her squirm.

Erebus slid his shadowy touch over Hestia. His cool caress stroked everywhere at once, igniting desire deep within her. She bit back the low moan that rose at his embrace.

His voice dropped to a hoarse whisper.

"Yes, I know. You do not want or need my help. Foolish child. You'd still be making the beds, sleepwalking through your days without me. You Olympians are as easy to goad as sheep."

The darkness shifted and solidified into the shape of a man, allowing dim light to penetrate the room. Featureless and made of shadow, Erebus lifted his hand and slipped his fingers beneath her chin. He ran his finger over her bottom lip, just as Apollo had the night before. Hestia swallowed and shivered an inferno of lust bloomed in her core. She sucked in a breath and her eyes went wide. Erebus leaned his shadow form close to her and skimmed a light kiss against her lips.

A cold hint of a breeze tickled her skin as he whispered, "The why is simple, my flame. You must burn because some lights are too bright to be hidden."

Katrina burst into the drying room, and the shadow figure dissipated, scattering itself to the corners once again. Hestia lifted her hand to cover her lips, where Erebus's cool touch still lingered.

"Here you are, My Lady. I'll see that the meal is served. Do you need me to dress your hair?" Katrina asked, handing Hestia a simple gown and veil.

Hestia took the bundle automatically and said, "No. I can manage. I'll be right behind you."

Katrina hesitated for a moment. "Are you alright? You're not yourself this morning." She laid her hand lightly on Hestia's arm and waited until Hestia met her gaze.

With a forced smile, Hestia waved away her concerns. "I didn't sleep well last night. I'm fine. Please be sure there are plenty of sweetmeats available."

Katrina nodded but didn't look convinced at Hestia's reassurance. Hestia sighed in relief when Katrina left without further questions. She had no answers to give her. Her mind slipped and slid over the events of the last day, trying to sift them into order, but shadows crept in, obscuring everything.

Hestia twisted the bundle of clothes in her hands until she gave up with a frustrated sigh. She needed to get on with her day and be busy with her duties. Marriage proposals and sensual shadow aside, she had a court to run, and it was time to get to it.

She looked around the tiny room. The shadows seemed to be only shadows, but Erebus could still be lurking. She flooded the small room with light, hoping he had lingered and now felt the burn. With not a shadow to be seen, she changed and hurried from the room, leaving her veil behind.

L ovely Hestia. Her fire burns so clearly. This Age of Olympia disappoints me. Gone are the great wars when gods acted like gods. The Olympians created mortals, who scurry like ants over the land. The Gods use them as pieces in a game. The great Olympians lounge on their mountain top and bicker and quarrel, consumed by *their petty intrigues. Hestia is far too good for them, but now they've noticed her. She will soon have to choose, and I shall go back to my corners and crevices, knowing that she will light the world revered as the goddess she is.*

I wonder if she will thank me.

SEVEN

Hestia walked into the banquet hall. A hush fell over the assembly, and all eyes turned toward her. Heat rose in her cheeks. She forced herself not to turn and run back to the kitchens. No one ever noticed when she came into a room.

As everyone stared, she noticed her bare face. Feeling naked and awkward, she hesitated near the entry. Athena, dressed in her customary breastplate and greaves, caught Hestia's eye. She lifted her chin and pulled her shoulders back in a soldier's posture. With a small smile, Hestia followed her lead.

"I hope everyone is enjoying their meal," Hestia said loud enough to carry across the room as she strolled through the assembly to the head table where Zeus sat. All the gods paid their respects to their king upon entering the room. Silence reigned as Hestia bowed to Zeus and Hera on the dais. "Is everything to your liking?" Hestia inquired, as she did every morning. Her voice sounded loud in the quiet room. She wished everyone would stop staring at her and go about their business.

"Of course, Sister. As always, we are so lucky to have such an able mistress managing our court." Zeus proclaimed it in his thundering voice, and a chorus of agreement broke out behind her.

The King of the Gods beckoned her to join him on the dais and waited until the assembly eventually picked up their conversation and utensils.

In a low tone, he continued, "You've caused quite a stir. Have you made your choice yet?"

"Leave her be, Zeus," Hera chided. "This is no small decision for her. Let her make it in peace."

Hestia studied her sandals so she wouldn't roll her eyes at Hera's feigned concern.

"Indeed, Wife, but I wonder if she understands the ramifications of her choice." Zeus looked serious and worried. "She doesn't comprehend the court and their fickle alliances. She worries about making sure there are enough bottles of wine for the table and if the guest chambers are comfortable."

Hestia's temper flared. She felt the stir of fire in her chest, but kept the flames contained.

"I'm standing right here, Zeus, and I understand far more than wine and linens."

Zeus's eyebrows shot up at her retort, but with her duty done, she didn't linger to continue the conversation. She turned on her heel and made her way to the banquet table that was laden with heaps of food and ambrosia.

Uncertainty gnawed at her. Despite her assurances to the contrary, Hestia knew little about alliances or court politics. What had Zeus meant by ramifications of her choice? Besides herself, Apollo, and Poseidon, who cared who she wed beyond having a new piece of gossip to fight over like the kitchen dogs over a scrap of meat?

Distracted and unsettled, Hestia put a few figs and grapes on her plate and turned to run right into Poseidon's muscular chest. He caught the plate deftly and wrapped an arm around her waist to pull her close to him.

"Did you rest well, my dear?" His voice rumbled low with the depths of the sea.

Hestia looked up at his chiseled features as her hands settled naturally on his chest. He smelled like fresh surf, and his gray eyes held the same tenderness as the night before. By the Fates, he actually seemed to care about her comfort and well-being. She smiled up at him.

"I slept like a baby," Hestia lied smoothly.

She wouldn't let him know that he and Apollo had stolen her sleep and peace of mind. She might be a novice at court intrigues, but she knew better than to appear weak in front of another god.

Poseidon squeezed her close to him, pressing her against his hard body, and dropped a kiss on the top of her head.

"I am pleased to hear it. I, too, slept well. You filled my dreams with your sweetness and in the early hours of the morning, I tasted your flames."

Hestia's stomach flipped, but she squirmed away from his embrace.

"Who sounds like a poet now?" she quipped and smiled at him.

Poseidon ran his hand through his hair. The tenderness in his eyes evaporated with irritation and embarrassment.

"Do not mock me," he growled in a low undertone.

Hestia laughed at the fragile egos of gods. "Don't worry, my Lord of the Sea. I won't tell anyone you have the heart of a poet under those barnacles."

She took her plate from him and walked away, marveling at the power of words. She realized why the court spent so much time sparring with each other, hurling jokes, barbs, and insults. Putting a pin prick in Poseidon's monumental ego filled her with a head rush of power, but she wasn't sure she liked it.

EIGHT

Hestia scanned the room. Gods, goddesses, demigods, and magical creatures mingled and meandered around the enormous hall. Aphrodite sat shamelessly in Ares's lap, feeding him grapes. The Muses gathered in a corner with a group of Oceanids chattering about last night's juicy bits of gossip, namely Hestia. Dionysus and Hephaestus sat apart from everyone else, eating and saying little, while Athena, Artemis, and Demeter carried on an animated discussion about the upcoming harvest festivals.

Hestia started toward Dionysus and Hephaestus. She had few real friends in the world, but the God of Wine and the God of the Forge both were on the list. They were outsiders in the world of Olympus. Hestia understood what that felt like, and they never overlooked her or her efforts.

Hestia hadn't taken a dozen steps when Iris reached out a delicate hand to stop her as she passed by. "Hestia, you must choose Apollo. He will be a good husband to you. I could listen to his poetry forever." Iris sighed and looked dreamy, considering Apollo and his poetry. Of course, as Hera's messenger, Iris would echo her mistress's opinion.

"Nay, Poseidon is the obvious choice," Hermes argued. He pointed at Hestia. "She doesn't want poetry. She wants power. Isn't that right, Hestia?"

Hestia flashed a grin. "Maybe I'll have them both."

Hermes, Iris, and everyone else close enough to hear sat in stunned silence for a heartbeat before erupting in laughter. Catcalls and lewd remarks followed her as she made her way to her friends. Half mortified and half exuberant, she sat down next to Hephaestus and stared at her plate. Neither of the gods said anything.

Finally, Dionysus broke the silence. "Enjoying yourself?" he asked. His tone dripped with disapproval.

Hestia swallowed and lifted her eyes. Dionysus regarded her sternly for a moment, before his mouth turned up in a grin. "Good for you, Hestia. You deserve a little fun."

Hephaestus chuckled and shook his head. "If this is your idea of fun, Dionysus, we need to get you off Olympus more often."

Hestia giggled, feeling the weight of decision lift in the company of her friend. It didn't last long. She might sound like a confident goddess with her witty remarks, but her heart twisted and turned like a sheet in the wind.

"I don't know what to do." Her voice sounded small and fragile.

She chewed her lip and looked back down at her plate. She wished she had Hera's determination or Athena's strength. She longed for Aphrodite's confidence, that everyone would love her no matter what. In the end, she was just plain Hestia, who made sure the bread was baked, and the beds were made.

Hephaestus laid one of his heavy, calloused hands on her leg beneath the table and squeezed gently. "You'll know what's right when it's time. You don't have to decide right away, though I doubt your suitors will be content to wait for long."

Hestia leaned against Hephaestus's sturdy shoulder, feeling like a miserable child who got in trouble even though she had done nothing wrong.

Dionysus looked at her from across the table with a grim expression. "You know there will be a fall out whatever you choose."

Hestia's brows drew together. Zeus had said something similar. She had no idea what they were talking about. Dionysus nodded as her confusion reflected in her expression.

"Oh, Hestia, your innocence becomes you, but you cannot play this game in ignorance. They are already dividing their allegiances." Dionysus gestured to encompass everyone in the room. "They are choosing who they will back in the war."

"War? What war?" Hestia exclaimed and sat up with a start, jostling the plates and goblets on the table and earning a few curious glances from those around them.

"Do you think either Apollo or Poseidon will just stand by and let the other one take what they have laid claim to? Not even you can be that blind. There will be retaliation. Everyone will choose a side, dividing Olympus right down the middle." Dionysus spoke in low and urgent, leaning toward her across the table.

Hestia's spirits plummeted even further as Dionysus laid bare the ramifications of her choice. Nothing was simple when it came to allegiances among the gods. This wasn't a game of words, of jests and jibes made in the great hall. The gods would pick up arms, and they would fight rather than suffer dishonor.

Her stomach churned, and Hestia wondered if Erebus had foreseen this. War and unrest were born of darkness. Maybe this was what he had intended the whole time.

Hestia slumped forward and buried her face in her hands. What she would give to turn back the hands of time and never set foot in that cursed cave. Hephaestus rubbed his hand up and down her back, soothing her.

"Don't lay all that on her shoulders. She isn't to blame if this lot wants to fight like two cats in a sack. They have nothing better to do than to gossip and squabble amongst themselves." Hephaestus's voice held contempt and disgust. His lip lifted in disdain as he sneered at the oblivious gods and goddesses around them.

"But it won't stay contained to Olympus, and you know it. It will spill over into the mortal realm and consume the entire world." Dionysus took a drink of his wine and crossed his arms with finality over his chest.

"Since when are you an Oracle, Dionysus? Stick to your grapes," Hephaestus snapped and glared at his friend. "You do what you think is right, Hestia."

Dionysus shook his head with a disgusted look. "You're not helping by coddling her." His features softened and he reached across the table to lay hand on Hestia's arm. "My dear, I don't mean to scare you. I just want you to know all the possibilities."

Hestia raised her head and looked back and forth between her friends. More confused than ever, she blinked back tears and pushed to her feet. "I think I'll go check on things in the kitchen. At least there, things make sense." She rushed from the hall before anyone else could speak to her.

Outside the kitchens, Apollo lounged in the doorway,

twirling a lily between his fingers. He smiled softly at her as she approached. Hestia stopped her headlong flight and stood self-consciously in the passageway. She swiped her hand across her face, erasing the tears that had spilled over. She looked at the Archer Prince where he stood, looking almost boyish. All the stars in the heavens couldn't compete with his perfection.

"I knew you'd turn up here, eventually. That mob in there is enough to drive you mad."

Hestia smiled weakly and nodded. "Did you break your fast? I can get you some sweetmeats from the kitchen if you like." She knew all the gods' favorite foods.

"You don't have to wait on me, Hestia." He closed the distance between them and tucked the lily in her hair. "The poor lily. Its beauty pales next to yours." His fingers brushed the side of her face, causing an avalanche of heat to pour through her.

Hestia's head spun. "Would you go to war if I chose Poseidon?" she blurted, swatting his hand away.

Apollo jerked back and looked down at her with a frown. "I would do anything to have you as my wife."

"I was afraid you would say that," Hestia murmured.

She pushed past him into the kitchens, but didn't stop there. She needed space and time to think. Better yet, she needed someone to talk to who understood these things but didn't have an agenda. She needed to find Themis, Goddess of Justice and Wisdom. Zeus often sought her counsel when he was wrestling with affairs of state. If anyone could help her, Themis could.

I t's almost too easy. I pulled one little thread, and the whole cloth unraveled in my hands. They're milling around, plotting and planning, as if they matter in the universe. They know not the power of the void, the place of nothing that holds the potential for everything. They cannot comprehend anything beyond the definitions of the world they created. Narrow-minded fools.

I wonder what will happen. Who will Hestia choose? Will she bring Olympus to its knees? Perhaps that would be best. Stiffen their spines and make real gods out of them.

I could help her, my bright goddess. From the ashes, she would rise a queen. She and I could rule supreme over the dark and the light. The shadow and the flame united. What a glorious age that would be.

NINE

Hestia slipped away from the palace as the sun rose high overhead. She took a little-used path that wound down the side of the mountain. Themis lived apart from the main court, rarely making appearances among the assembly. Themis claimed living among the other gods clouded her vision and swayed her judgment. Hestia had never spoken more than a word of welcome to the Titan and had always been more than a little in awe of the austere goddess.

Just above the cloud line, Hestia saw the tiny stone house with a small courtyard. It looked tidy and quaint, not at all what Hestia had imagined. She had assumed Themis would live in a marble palace like Zeus and Hera, as befitted her station. Unpretentious and simple, Themis's house could have been a dwelling in the mortal village at the base of Olympus.

Hestia knocked on the sturdy wooden door and waited. She couldn't believe it when Themis herself opened the door. Didn't she have any servants?

Gathering her wits, Hestia bowed low to the Titan and

said, "Lady Themis! I hope I'm not intruding, but I'm in desperate need of your wisdom."

Themis stood with a simple gown of gleaming white trimmed in gold. Her sharp green eyes stood out with her ebony hair pulled severely back from her face. She looked down her nose at Hestia and took in her fiery red hair and simple dress. Her lips pressed into a disapproving frown.

"I do not embroil myself in court intrigues. I cannot tell you how to win his heart. Wisdom is not needed in choosing a bed partner. Wisdom concerns itself with the mind, not the heart."

Themis made to close the door, but Hestia straightened up and stepped forward, blocking the doorway.

"That's exactly why I need your help! I can't sort out my head from my heart. Please," Hestia paused and bit her lip. "I need someone who doesn't have their own interests to advance. As you said, you care nothing for court intrigues. That makes you the perfect person to help me."

Themis pursed her lips. "You've made a logical case. Come in, Hestia, and let us see what can be done for you."

Themis knew all about of the developments of the last several days, but she asked Hestia to recount the story from her point of view. When Erebus entered the story, the ancient Titan stopped her.

"The Lord of the Darkness has emerged from the deep?"

Hestia nodded, and Themis's implacable expression shifted to one of concern. She rose swiftly and stood over a plain stone basin of water. She passed her hand over the mirror-like surface. Hestia craned her neck to see, but all she could make out was shifting shadows, followed by a bright flash of light.

Themis turned to her, giving Hestia a hard, appraising

look. Her severe mouth pressed into a thin line. "My informants couldn't tell me what had stirred the hornet's nest. I thought you had taken a notion that you wanted a bit of attention for yourself. But it wasn't you, was it?"

"No! I never sought any of this. It just happened. I was feeling a bit underappreciated and melancholy," Hestia confessed and dropped her gaze to the floor under the disapproving stare of Themis.

The Titan spoke, seemingly to herself. "She is the Goddess of Hearth and Home. She commands fire, the most powerful element. Yet, she uses it to bring comfort and light. She is not a conqueror. She is a peacemaker and a homemaker. Every mortal that walks in our realm makes offerings first to her, above all others. She is powerful but does not seek to use that power." Themis fell silent. She tapped her finger on her lips while staring at the wall, lost in contemplation.

Hestia waited for her to continue. She twisted her skirt in her fingers while the seconds grew into minutes. She crossed her ankles, uncrossed them, and crossed them again. She fidgeted and sighed, but Themis seemed to have forgotten she was there. Aggravated with herself as much as Themis, she stood and smoothed her skirt. She paced and stared at the small courtyard through the window.

Apollo's kiss and Poseidon's powerful embrace played in her mind. The shadows grew longer as Hestia waited. The black shapes on the stones brought Erebus and his silky, cool caress to mind. She leaned her head against the stone wall, wrestling to hold her tongue and her patience in check. Her head pounded and her fingers drummed on the window. The silence broke her eventually, and she whirled around to face Themis.

"Is this your great wisdom? Stay silent until I decide for

myself?" Themis's gaze never left the spot on the wall she had been staring at for the last hour. Bitter resentment boiled over, and Hestia no longer cared to contain it. "So, this is it? There will be no husband for me. There will no great romance, no passion, no love." Her voice cracked and her hands balled into fists. Anger threatened to choke her, but now that she had given voice to her true feelings, she would not be silent. Through clenched teeth, she continued her tirade. "Aphrodite and Zeus hop from bed to bed, and no one threatens to go to war over them! For once, someone paid attention to me, and it's going to destroy everything I hold dear. What did I ever do to the fates to deserve this?"

Tears stung her eyes, and Hestia tried to blink them back. Weeping served no purpose. She pulled in a deep breath and fought for her cool, detached control. A single tear escaped and trickled down her cheek. Themis, who hadn't even flinched during Hestia's outburst, shot out her hand and caught the tear on her finger. Muttering to herself, Themis returned to the basin of water and touched the tear to the surface.

Hestia held her breath as light rose from the water's surface. It danced and swayed, bathing Themis's angular face in shadows and stared fixedly at the swirling visions before her. The light evaporated, and Themis turned to Hestia with a grave look.

"You will not like what I have to say."

Themis's words fell like hammer blows. Hestia bit her lip and willed herself not to cry. She lifted her chin and met the Titan's intense green eyes.

"Say what you will. I came to hear it and will not shy away now."

"Very well, but you must know that I cannot see the future. My daughters, the Fates, have given me only a glimpse of what may come. One thing I can tell you for certain, Olympus will fall if you choose the Earth Shaker or the Archer Prince."

The ominous warning hung in the air. Hestia's stomach dropped to her toes, and she turned to the window, fighting for control. Fire churned in her belly as rage like she had never felt surged within her. Why did she deserve such a destiny? Why must she live her life alone, never knowing the love of a husband or the touch of a lover? The injustice scorched her soul.

She bowed low to hide her fury. Angry though she was, she would not insult the Titan or embarrass herself further. Through the tightness in her throat, she choked out, "Very well, Wise One. I will refuse them both and stay a maiden forever."

"I was not finished," Themis snapped. "I have no patience for dramatic goddesses."

Hestia straightened up and met Themis's sharp gaze. With an effort, she let go of some of her bitterness and bowed her head respectfully. "Forgive me. It has been a difficult morning."

Themis waved her words away, and a glint of mischief entered her eyes. "The Fates acknowledge you have been ensnared in an intrigue not of your own making. They offer you one night to escape your destiny. In two nights time, you will host a celebration. All who attend must conceal their identity. You may choose a consort on this night and this night only, but you must make your choice with your heart, not your eyes."

Hestia's mind scrambled to adjust. "If I cannot tell one god from the next, how will I know who to choose?"

Themis smiled at her. "That is the first worthy question

you have asked me. Your choice should be the one who begins where you end."

Hestia sighed and looked out the window, weary from the day's turmoil. She pushed to her feet and bowed deeply to Themis. "Very well. I appreciate your counsel and will do my best to heed it."

When she straightened, Themis wore a soft expression. "Hestia, yours is not a glamorous role. You do not shine like Aphrodite or wield power like Hera or Athena. However, never underestimate your importance. You are the balance, the equilibrium, that unites them all, and in that, my dear, you hold the ultimate power."

Themis turned her attention back to the stone basin, passing her hand over its shimmering surface.

Hestia let herself out and considered Themis's words as she walked toward the palace. Could she content herself with one night? Surely it was a better option than choosing a husband and toppling Olympus into a war.

Hestia picked up a rock and flung it, sending her resentment and anger away with. She could not go against the Fates. She was the invisible goddess, and her place was among the shadows. She'd have to make the most of her one night.

*T*he Moirai have spoken. They understand she needs to burn, but true to their miserly ways, offer her just one night. Is that enough for this bright flame? Will the world remember her with a single night? No, it is not enough. They cannot confine a fire such as hers to a solitary, brief flash.

The three all-seeing sisters, who hold the power of time,

life, and prophecy, do not look to the past, only the future. They have forgotten me. They spin webs of fortune and fate, but their words do not bind me. I existed before them, limitless, everlasting. Their decree does not bind me. They give her a night. I can give her eternity.

Can she see beyond the darkness? Is she brave enough to take the chance?

TEN

Hestia's thoughts ran round and round as she walked back to the palace, as she wrestled to find acceptance of her fate. She jumped and gave a startled cry when Hermes materialized in front of her.

"I've been calling your name, Hestia. Did you not hear me?" The messenger god floated a few inches off the ground as the wings on his sandals fluttered.

"I'm sorry. I've got a lot on my mind. What do you need? Did you get the oranges I sent to your room? They were the last of the season." Hestia kept all the gods stocked with their favorite treats.

"I did indeed. They're the sweetest and juiciest I've ever tasted." Hermes moved to the side and joined Hestia as she made her way down the trail. "Why do you walk like a common mortal? You have the power to travel any way you choose, but you plod along like you're stuck to the earth."

"It suits me, I guess," Hestia answered after considering for a moment. "I like to feel connected to the earth and the life force that comes from it. I'll let you do the flying." She smiled at Hermes, who did a graceful flip in the air. "Why were you looking for me," she asked, already guessing the answer.

"Zeus wants to speak to you. He wants to know who you've chosen. You could tell me, and I'll take the message to him," Hermes offered, trying to sound innocent.

Hestia knew better than to fall for that. She wasn't ready to reveal her half-made plans to anyone, but if she told Hermes, the entire court would know before she even got back to the palace. The mischievous god had a well-earned reputation for sharing secrets that were not his to share.

Hestia shook her head. "I'll see Zeus myself. Thank you for delivering the message."

Hermes shrugged his shoulder and waved as he ascended into the sky and disappeared.

Hestia reached the outskirts of the palace grounds. The walk had done little to settle her mind, so instead of seeking Zeus, she ducked into the shade of an almond tree.

Weariness weighed on her as she leaned back against the tree. Her sleepless night and the stress of the day made her feel ancient and feeble. Her overwhelmed mind stuttered to a halt, too tired to keep turning the same thoughts over and over again, hoping for a different outcome.

The shade cut the intensity of the afternoon's heat. A cool breeze blew across her face, and Hestia's eyelids drooped. She didn't resist sleep as it stole over her, shutting out the world with comforting nothingness.

The song of the maiden echoed in her head. Hestia twirled round and round, floating on air, dancing in the clouds. Apollo lifted and swung her around. He pulled her close, nuzzling her next. She expected the heat and hardness of his body, but only cool emptiness met her. As his mouth descended to meet hers, he dissolved in shadow.

Propelled by the music, she turned, swirling mists around her, weightless and free. Poseidon offered his hand. He caught her by the wrist and pressed a kiss to her palm. She felt nothing as he, too, evaporated into smoky wisps.

Blackness enveloped her. Silky and solid, the cool caress pressed against her, sliding sensually over her body. Desire unfurled within her. Light flare to life and Hestia saw herself as elemental fire, burning white-hot and glorious.

Shadows, cold against her heat, danced around her as her flames flickered and burned. A desperate longing surged through her as the fire and shadow danced. The flame ebbed and flickered, and the shadow leapt. Undulating, circling, chasing, the flame and the shadow went on and on, never meeting, never merging, never together. Crushing loneliness clawed at her. The fire guttered, and all was black.

Hestia gasped as she jerked awake. Her skin tingled, chilled and covered in goosebumps. She blinked her eyes. She knew they were open, but she could see nothing in the impenetrable darkness. Heart-rending loneliness clawed at her, and the cool shadows faded, sliding reluctantly away.

The daylight returned and she scrambled to her feet. Hestia pulled in a deep breath as the sunshine warmed her skin but did nothing to banish the deep unease that lingered. The shadow dance played in her mind. Somehow, she'd seen through the shadow's eyes, felt his needs. The loneliness belonged to the shadow. It hungered for the flame, but the two could never be one.

The dream played over and over in her mind, leaving her uneasy. Hestia couldn't put her finger on it, but something eluded her as she sorted through the events of the last day. Erebus had set everything in motion. That she was sure of. But why? Hestia suspected boredom had instigated his actions, but something had changed. The shadow man in the herb room hadn't bored. Desire and need drove the darkness that danced with her flame in her dream. Somehow, she and Erebus had come together in that dreamscape, though she didn't think he had intended it.

Pity filled her as she walked toward the assembly hall to find Zeus. Welcomed at any hearth in the world, mortals and gods revered her light. Erebus was welcome nowhere and banished at every opportunity. She wondered what she could do to help him.

Hestia sighed as she slipped into the palace. The cool air of the marble hall refreshed her flushed skin. She put the God of Darkness out of her mind. He would have to wait until after she dealt with the mess he had made.

Gods and goddesses lounged in the great hall. Whispers erupted and low conversations buzzed as she crossed to the dais.

Going through the motions automatically, she bowed to Zeus.

"Have you decided then, sister?"

Hestia's mouth went dry, and her heart hammered in her chest. She turned to face the assembly and raised her voice.

"I have spoken to Themis," she announced, and everyone in the chamber went still. No one wanted to miss a word.

Zeus's eyebrows rose in surprise, but he nodded his approval. "You were wise to seek her counsel. This was far too big of a decision for you to make on your own. Who did she tell you to choose?"

Hestia's temper flared, and a flicker of flame danced around her for a moment. A gasp ran through the host. With an effort, she clamped down on her emotions. Her hands curled into fists, and she infused an icy edge in her voice.

"I am perfectly capable of making any decision I need to." Hestia lifted her chin. With a steady voice, she proclaimed, "There will be a masked ball held in two days. Everyone is welcome to attend, but you must conceal your identity or risk offending the Fates. I will announce my decision at that time."

Without another word, she swept from the hall as a babble of voices and calls for explanation chased her. A small smile played at her lips. Let them gossip and guess. She might be destined for invisibility, but it didn't mean she had to go quietly.

∿

These infants know nothing. A masquerade to hide their faces? More games for children!

I showed her the shadow and the flame. I brought her into the light, and she pities me?

How can she pity the one who knows no limits? How dare she feel sorry for me, like it matters that these simpletons do not welcome me with open arms? Foolish, ignorant child.

There are dangers in the darkness, and she should not forget that.

I do not want her pity. I do not need her concern. I did this for her, but she is as blind as the others. I will leave her to her games and let the fates bind her. It matters not to me.

ELEVEN

As gods and demigods poured in from all corners of the world to attend the masquerade, Olympus resembled more of a zoo than the high court of the gods. No god wanted to be outdone, so they all traveled with an entourage of servants and animals to prove their wealth and standing. It made Hestia's job of preparing meals, music, and accommodation that much harder.

Hestia examined the tear in the hem of her gown, a result of breaking up a fight between her mother's lions and Hecate's pack of hounds. Hecate, the Goddess of Witchcraft and Magic, threatened to change the lions into kittens if they didn't leave her hounds alone.

"Just keep the lions outside, mother," Hestia ground out between clenched teeth.

Rhea, Hestia's mother, shrugged and petted the lion's massive head. "Those curs of Hecate's slink around in the shadows and upset everyone. They're always watching."

Hestia took a deep breath. "They're the Watchers of Time, mother. What do you expect them to do? And it's not just the dogs. Your pets make everyone nervous. Please keep them outside or in your chambers. I've set up a lovely corner of the garden just for them."

"Hestia," a woman's voice called from behind her.

Hestia whirled around with a smile blossoming on her face. "Persephone!" She waved across the milling crowds. "No more lions in the hall, mother," she reminded before she hurried toward her friend.

Persephone, the Queen of Hell, threw her arms around Hestia's neck. "It's so good to see you and I can't thank you enough for giving me a reason to get into the light for a while." She pulled back and looked at Hestia with concern. "What in the name of the fates has gotten into you?"

Hestia laughed and shook her head. "It wasn't me. It all started when I went for a walk and—"

"I'm so sorry to interrupt, but you're needed, my lady," Katrina slipped up next to Hestia and murmured in her ear.

Hestia closed her eyes for a moment. The last two days had been nothing but managing one crisis after another. She would give anything for a bit of peace.

"Of course. I'll be right there," she murmured to Katrina. "I'll tell you everything just as soon as I can find five minutes to myself," she promised Persephone and she hurried after her paige. She returned pleasantries as she wove through the crowd and gave Hades a brief hug as she rushed past.

On the wide east portico, Hestia stumbled to stop next to Katrina.

"Oh no. Dionysus," she called and looked over the crowd in a frantic search for the God of Wine. "Find him and bring him here, quickly," Hestia instructed Katrina and pushed her back into the crowd.

Hestia's all-inclusive invitation had traveled throughout the land. Magical creatures flocked to Olympus in answer to the rare opportunity to participate in the celebration. Centaurs, giants, nymphs, and even a few harpies had arrived. They had no need for masks and had been a great help in getting things ready. Hestia found giants were particularly handy for hanging garlands and clearing a path through the crowd.

The group of satyrs that climbed up the final few stairs of the portico on the other hand promised to be anything but helpful. Indulgent, fun-loving, and lustful, the satyrs loved to dance, drink, and make love. They brought a party with them wherever they went and could turn Hestia's one magical evening into an out-of-control orgy. Dionysus was the only one she knew who could exert any control over them.

A tall satyr with olive colored skin and thick glossy black curls approached her. The tips of his horns peeked through his hair and his horse tail trailed behind him. Wearing only a loin cloth that did little to disguise what lay beneath, his freshly oiled bare skin shone in the sunlight. He bowed to her.

"Lady Hestia. I am Jiel. My brothers and I are honored to join your celebration." He stood and smiled.

Hestia's stomach did a flip and her cheeks flushed as her core clenched in response to his smile. He smelled so good, sweet like honeysuckle mixed with cedar. His gaze roamed over her, leaving a tingling trail of heat.

"Jiel, stop!" Dionysus's command cut through the haze that filled Hestia's mind.

She blinked and found herself pressed against the hard body of the satyr. With a gasp, she pushed away. Jiel grinned lazily at her. His brown eyes flashed with the promise of passion, and she gasped again as a shot of liquid heat lanced through her. Her nipples contracted and she bit her lip against the moan of desperate need that seized her like an iron fist.

"Stop," Dionysus said again, grabbing Jiel's arm.

Jiel held up his hands in surrender. "I can't help it. She's delicious." He flicked an unapologetic glance over Hestia and licked his lips.

"You're going to have to leave," Dionysus growled and pulled the satyr down the stairs.

"Wait!" Hestia hurried to block their path. "I meant it when I said everyone was invited. I know how it feels to be left out."

Dionysus stopped and gave her a sad look. He also knew the feeling all too well.

"Jiel, do you promise to keep your influences to yourself until after I've made my choice?" Hestia asked.

Jiel pouted. "Well, it won't be much of a party, but if you insist, we'll behave. What about after you make your choice?"

"Once my choice is made, the night is yours." Hestia winked and turned away.

One more crisis solved.

"Hestia!" Aphrodite's shrill call reached her. With a sigh, Hestia turned to face her next challenge.

TWELVE

Hours later, Hestia slipped into her chambers, avoiding a group of Oceanids. Poseidon sent them to wheedle their way into her confidence. She didn't know how the others played these endless court games. She found them exhausting. With a sigh, she dropped into a chair and closed her eyes for a moment. She was officially done organizing and planning. The masquerade started in an hour, and she needed to get ready.

"Hestia, I'd like a word," Zeus announced as he entered her room without permission. Zeus never knocked. As the King of the Gods, he would go where he wanted.

Hestia didn't open her eyes or stir from her chair. "What do you want, Zeus? Everything is going to be fine. I'm not going to upend Olympus into a war. Please leave me be." Her tone would have frozen the blood of a mortal man, but it bounced off Zeus unnoticed.

"I will not leave you be until you tell me your intentions. It has been my experience that goddesses' intrigues do not always end the way they intend." Zeus's voice rumbled with displeasure.

"I told you. I have a plan. The Fates told me what I must do." Hestia tried one more time to deflect Zeus's question, but even before the words left her, she knew he was not to be dissuaded.

She cracked her eyes open and glared at him as he towered over her with his arms crossed and a ferocious scowl on his face. Lightning flashed in his eyes. Hestia threw her hands up and pushed herself out of the chair.

"Fine, Zeus! However, I will have a promise from you before I reveal my plans."

She stood with her hands on her hips and chin held high in defiance, a posture she'd seen Hera use a hundred times.

Zeus stared at her a moment, nonplussed before he shrugged and dropped into the chair Hestia had vacated.

"Name your terms, Sister." He kept his tone cordial. Now that he was getting what he wanted, he didn't need to rumble and threaten. Zeus lounged in the chair and looked at her expectantly.

In that moment, Hestia hated him. Zeus always got his way. He sacrificed nothing for the greater good. He never denied himself any pleasure or desire. The unfairness of the world simmered within her, stirring her flames that burned close to the surface. With an effort, she tamped down her aggravation and forced her mind to focus on her demands.

"I want the hearth offerings of Olympus," Hestia declared and smiled at Zeus's shocked look.

As Goddess of the Hearth, she already received all the mortal hearth offerings, but there were offerings made directly to Olympus that went to Zeus. Giving them to Hestia would do nothing to weaken his power, but it would add considerably to hers.

Zeus recovered quickly. "This is no small thing. What do you intend to do with them? I never thought you were power-hungry like the rest of them."

There was a trace of disappointment in his eyes that made her feel guilty for a moment. Then, she remembered all she was sacrificing in the name of keeping the peace. She would not walk away from this with only a night of memories.

"I don't plan to do anything other than what I have always done. Do I not earn them? Am I not the one who keeps this house and home?" Hestia demanded, and didn't bother to quell her flames. They danced around her feet, rising quickly to her knees.

Zeus put his hands up in a placating gesture. "You've made your point. There's no need to roast me in my chair." He regarded her for a moment before shaking his head with a wry laugh. "You're full of surprises, Hestia. No wonder you've got gods fighting for your hand. Very well. The hearth offerings of Olympus are yours. Now, tell me your plan."

The fire died as Hestia sat primly on the edge of her bed. She was getting better at court intrigues. After extracting a promise of secrecy, she told Zeus what the Fates had revealed to Themis.

"So, tonight is my night, and tomorrow I will announce that I will remain unmarried forever."

Zeus nodded. "It's a good plan, but be sure to choose wisely. The Fates do not give second chances." He stood and looked down at her. "I don't know what prompted this change, but you will not be overlooked so easily in the future. Enjoy your night, Hestia."

A loud squawk of a raven punctuated his exit, and the

huge, black bird took off from the olive tree outside her window. A feather drifted in and landed on the floor at her feet. Hestia picked it up and brushed it down her cheek as she pulled out her gown and veil. It was time to get ready for the party.

THIRTEEN

Gods, goddesses, demigods, and magical creatures crowded into the assembly hall. Tonight, Hestia was just one of the host. For the first time, she had no responsibilities. Feeling like she wasn't quite connected to the ground, euphoria at the potential the night held swelled in her chest. This was her night, her chance, and she was going to make the most of it.

Hestia moved along with the crowd, trying to look everywhere at once. Masks of brilliant shining gold and silver hid faces. Some masks had feathers, flowers, and jewels to add to the mystery. Crowns, veils, and elaborate headdresses complimented robes and gowns of every color in the rainbow.

A live snake coiled on top of a man's head like a turban. Hestia wondered how he convinced the creature to stay perched there. A woman slid through the crowd wearing a costume made entirely of butterflies. They clung to her with their wings outspread, making a breathtaking pattern. Hestia resisted the temptation to startle them and see if they would all take flight, leaving no doubt to what a goddess wore beneath her gown.

Hestia worked her way to the edge of the crowd. She wanted to find a corner where she could watch and consider her choice. Her shadow silk gown swished around her ankles, and she marveled again at the enchanted fabric.

Years ago, Hestia had taken pity on Arachne, the woman Athena turned into a spider, and gave her refuge in a broom closet. She sought the spider's help to weave a special cloth for the masquerade. Arachne used shadow and moonlight with her spider silk to create a fabric that was lighter than air. Hestia could barely feel the gown against her skin. Her veil, made of the same material, concealed her fiery curls, and she draped it across her face, revealing only her eyes. If she stood still, she became almost invisible, like a smudge of shadow.

Hestia found the perfect corner and stood close to an enormous potted fern. She looked out over the crowd and the difficulty of her choice became clear. The assembly hall swarmed with activity, making it hard for her to single out anyone—especially the one she wanted to name her consort. How was she to choose with everyone constantly moving around?

Despite the pressure of her situation, Hestia bit back a giggle when she recognized Hephaestus's unsteady gait and took in his outrageous costume. In a mocking homage to his wife, he wore a wig of blond hair that tumbled over his shoulders, and his broad chest stretched a diaphanous white gown to its limits. A sheer white veil disguised his face, except for his eyes that he had outlined with charcoal. His painted red lips matched Aphrodite's and showed through the sheer fabric. Gold armbands shaped like roses snaked up his forearms.

Hestia admired his handy work until she saw the roses were strangling a swan. Poor Hephaestus. He was married to the Goddess of Love, who had no love for him. Hestia sighed sadly, her heart squeezing for her friend's unhappiness as he secured a bottle of wine from Dionysus and retired to a corner of his own to watch the spectacle.

Hera was likewise easy to identify. Wearing a gown of spectacular peacock feathers and a mask adorned with diamonds, sapphires, and emeralds, she swept through the throng with a white peacock on a leash. Hestia pitied the poor bird and wondered if there was a flock of naked peacocks running around Olympus.

Athena and Demeter had chosen less ostentatious outfits. Hestia smiled as her sisters elbowed their way through the crowd. They wore their maiden gowns, just as they did every other day. Athena looked ready to lead an army onto the field of battle with her breastplate and greaves, and Demeter adorned her hair with a crown of wheat. They both had a simple silk mask to conceal their face and placate the fates, though their identity was far from secret.

Unfortunately, not everyone chose something so easily recognizable. Hestia tried to pick out Apollo or Poseidon, but none of the men she could see wore anything that gave a clue to their identity.

A centaur wandered past and stood in front of her, blocking her view. She used a fern frond to tickle his haunches until he spun around and glared at the offending plant. She stood still and melted into the shadow. The creature stared hard for a moment but then shrugged and moved on. Hestia resumed her observations, standing on her tip toes to see as much as she was able.

The Muses, all wearing simple masks across their eyes,

filed in and began to sing. The gods, goddesses, and creatures broke into lines and moved through the steps of the
dance. Hestia watched, enchanted by the swirling colors
and lilting melody.

"Is it everything you hoped it would be?"

FOURTEEN

H estia spun toward the voice. Apollo stood behind
her wearing a mask of black raven feathers and a
black cape. She knew him instantly. Nothing
could disguise his honeyed tones and crystal blue eyes. A
large black raven sat on his shoulder and tilted its head to
the side as if it had asked the question.

"It's overwhelming," she replied honestly, and the raven
gave a squawk as if in agreement before it beat its great
wings and took flight. Hestia watched it as it swooped over
the crowd before coming to rest on the head of a giant statue
of Zeus.

"It's all for you, and yet, here you are standing in a
corner in a gown that makes you almost invisible."

Apollo's words drew her attention back to him. He
looked down at her with those heartbreakingly blue eyes
that went smoky around the edges.

"As if a gown of shadows could hide your fire." He drew
in a breath and spoke in lilting verse. "Hestia, Goddess of
fire,

Keeper of the hearth and home,

Your light warms all those around you
Your goodness banishes the dark."

Apollo traced the back of his hand down her cheek, and molten fire erupted in her core. A small smile played across his lips as tiny flames flickered at the edge of her gown. She leaned into his caress, lost in his words.

"We never finished our dance," he whispered.

Before she could answer, Apollo slipped his arm around her and turned her deftly in time with the music. Hestia followed willingly, her heart tripping madly in her chest, and every nerve ending alight with excitement. She tried to keep the flames in check, but her emotions ran too hot. They danced in a bed of fire as Apollo steered them on to the portico.

The Antikristos began, and the familiar haunting melody played. Apollo pulled her tightly to him as he led them, spinning slowly around and around. Hestia pressed herself against him, feeling every inch of her body against his. Aching desire spread through her. Fire licked up to their knees, and Apollo laughed softly.

Apollo stopped their slow progress and lowered his mouth to hers. His kiss sent pleasure rioting through her. Flames danced around them, cocooning them in a nest of heat. The moment spun on, and Hestia could think of nothing else but the sheer bliss of his touch, his taste. Apollo dropped kisses down her neck, and she shivered with pleasure.

"I never knew you burned so hot. What a fool I was not to see it. It might be only for tonight, but as long as I have you once, I can be content with that," Apollo whispered as his hands roamed over her.

Like a bucket of cold water, Apollo's words hit her.

Hestia pushed away from him, and the flames evaporated, leaving her feeling cold and empty.

"What did you say?"

Her heart hammered in her chest. Only Zeus and Themis knew of the stipulations set by the Fates. She looked up at the Archer Prince and remembered the raven outside her window. Apollo had been eavesdropping.

He shrugged, unapologetic. "It wasn't fair to keep us waiting. Besides, one night is better than never. I promise I will make it a night that will keep you warm for eternity." He moved to take her in his arms again, but she sidestepped out of his reach.

"What's this?" Poseidon's deep voice came from behind her.

She whirled around to see the God of the Sea prowling onto the portico. A bone mask made from bull's head with enormous golden horns hid his face, but there was no mistaking the sound of the sea in his voice.

"One night? Is this more of your drivel, Poet?"

Apollo's mouth twisted into a sneer. "Do you have seaweed in your ears? That's what the Fates have decreed. No husband for our beautiful Hestia. She has but this one night to choose a consort. I'm surprised Zeus didn't tell you."

Poseidon's eyes flashed, and the ground shook beneath them. "One night or eternity. You'll not have her," the Sea God rumbled with all the power of the deep, and his trident materialized in his hand. Several masked creatures poured onto the portico and flanked Poseidon.

Apollo rolled his eyes theatrically. "You can shake the ground and throw a tantrum, but Hestia will be mine. She practically gave herself to me right here under your nose."

The Archer Prince removed his cape with a flourish. It

morphed into his golden bow, and a quiver of arrows appeared on his back. Confidently, he nocked an arrow and waited with his fingers resting loosely on the string. Behind him, several black-caped figures with raven masks closed in from the open end of the portico.

Hestia watched in horror as the two gods faced off. The music fell silent, and gods and goddesses flooded onto the portico, sorting themselves according to their allegiances. Swords and spears were drawn as the assembly readied itself for battle.

Artemis, Apollo's twin, joined him with her bow in hand. "Are you sure she's worth it, Brother?" she asked.

"That ancient sea slug will not have her. She will be mine," Apollo snapped, never taking his eyes away from Poseidon.

Artemis shrugged and drew an arrow from her quiver. Her contingent of maiden huntresses behind her followed suit.

Poseidon drove his trident into the marble tile of the portico. A tremor ran through the ground, opening a crack beneath their feet. "She'll be yours the day the oceans run dry," Poseidon retorted and flung off his bone mask. His hair flowed over his shoulders as wild as a tempest. Power radiated from him, and his trident sang the song of the sea.

Hestia placed herself between the gods, fuming with rage. "Enough!"

Her voice rang out, clear and sharp. Silence fell as everyone turned their attention to her. Fury roiled inside her, and she did nothing to dampen the flames that sprang up around her. They had spoiled everything. They professed to love her but cared nothing for her, except as a trophy to show their strength. Flames whipped higher, and her veil of shadows blew away. Her hair became flame as her elemental nature took hold. Her feet left the ground as the fire lifted her. Her eyes reflected the blaze, and when she spoke, her voice roared with the energy of the inferno.

"I am not yours for the taking. I am a goddess, born of the Titans, full of flame and fire. I am not some kitchen scrap to be fought over by arrogant boys. You disgust me. None of you are worthy of me!"

Hestia gathered handfuls of fire and flung them at Poseidon and Apollo, who cringed and ducked. Disappointment crashed over her, choking her fury in its icy grasp. As her heart shattered, the fireballs fizzled, and the flames receded beneath her. Her feet touched down on the cracked marble tiles and silence echoed in answer to her outburst.

Tears gathered in her eyes. Her one night, her one chance was gone, ruined at the hands of greedy gods. Exposed and disappointed, Hestia stood before her fellow gods and goddesses. Every eye fixed on her and the beautiful gown that hung in tatters around her. Her fiery curls drooped listlessly around her face.

Hephaestus and Dionysus elbowed their way through the crowd toward her, but she couldn't face them. Oh, how she wished she could be invisible again. With a sob, she turned and fled.

∿

I n the end, I could not stay away. I could not tuck myself into the hidden places of the earth and forget.

As I thought, these Olympians are not worthy of her. They cannot put aside their own selfish desires and see the treasure she is. I would destroy them all for the injury they have given her.

But, for now, she needs me, though she may not know it.

She awakened me, just as I awakened her.

Come to me, my Goddess of Fire. Bring me your shattered dreams and wounded soul.

I whisper to her in the shadows, and I wait, daring to hope.

FIFTEEN

Hestia ran through the garden and along the small path that led away from the palace. She stumbled through darkness as anger and embarrassment threatened to consume her.

The shadows whispered words like rustling leaves. Over her gasping breath and pounding heart, they hovered just beyond her understanding. Tears poured down her face as she ran blindly, slipping and sliding in the loose gravel. She slowed as she climbed higher among the boulders, and the way became steeper. The whispers grew louder, but she still strained to hear them.

Her sandal broke and she tripped. Rocks bit into her hands and knees. She crawled to a nearby boulder and leaned against it. The cool, rough surface rubbed against her skin, and she brushed away the gravel that clung to her bruised knees. Out of tears and lost in misery, she stared into the darkness.

"The flame creates the shadow."

The words came from all around her, hissing and

rustling. Hestia's heart pounded. There were dangers in the darkness, even for a goddess.

"Erebus?" she demanded of the darkness, but only rustling whispers answered her. "Show yourself, Dark One. Come and tell me of my folly. Come and laugh at my pain. You got what you wanted."

Anger at the meddlesome god flashed through her. Flames danced around her, illuminating the rocks and scrubby shrubs. Shadow crept over the ground and snuffed out the fires.

"The shadow cannot exist without light. Come to me, Goddess of Fire, Goddess of Kindness, Goddess of Good. Come to me and burn."

Her resentment faded as his words penetrated her wounded heart. She heard his call and remembered his touch. The shadow and the light bound together in the balance of eternity. How could she have been so blind?

"Come to me and burn." The shadows swirled around her.

Dim, undulating light beckoned to her through a crack in the rock face. Hestia scrambled to her feet, kicking out of her sandals. She didn't notice the sharpness of the rocks as she ran toward the light. Without hesitation, she slipped through the crevice and flung herself into the dark abyss.

Hestia's heartbreak and sorrow boiled over. Free-falling into the darkness, her anger and disappointment flowed freely. Flame consumed her as she gave herself over to her elemental form. Hestia became flame and fury, burning incandescent as she filled the void.

Erebus rose to meet her. He surrounded her with his vastness and cradled her as she raged. He took her anger, and with a kiss of shadow, quelled it. He absorbed her fury and returned gentle calm. She battered herself against him, and he stood stalwart, strong, and silent until she burned herself out. Then, with infinite tenderness, he rocked her.

Hestia stared into the darkness that surrounded her. As if every star, sun, and moon had been snuffed out, not a pinprick of light could be seen. Silence cocooned her, and a welcome sense of peace stole over her.

Suspended in the void, Hestia gave Erebus the broken shards of her hope, her heart, and her soul. He filled in the gaps and made them whole again. Darkness caressed her, suspended her weightless and bodiless in his infinite presence. His cool touch filled her with passion and love as she felt him coming alive. Her fire fed his shadows. Realization dawned, and she understood how wrong she had been about everything.

Erebus coiled around her, soothing, sheltering. His was not the darkness of strife, hate, or fear. He brought peace, quiet, and stillness. From him, the light had balance, and the world could rest under his protection. By the Fates, she had judged him without knowing. She, like everyone else, had painted him with the same brush as the other creatures of the night.

Without words, in a language older than speech, she apologized.

"My Love, forgive my ignorance and my sharp words. I see you now for what you are, and I will never forget."

"Hestia, fire of my soul and bringer of light, you helped me remember. Hidden away, I became the dark that people fear. I had lost my true self. Thank you for helping me remember."

Joy filled Hestia at his words. She found all that she ever dreamed of as she embraced the one who began where she ended. In the abyss, the shadow and the fire danced in slow harmony.

EPILOGUE

Hestia wandered back to the palace under the early rays of dawn. Dionysus and Hephaestus dozed in the southern gardens, propped against the very fig tree Zeus had hidden behind only a few short days ago. She smiled when she saw them and gently shook them awake.

"Where have you been all night?" Hephaestus asked. His words slurred slightly as he lurched to his feet and scrubbed a hand over his face. "We waited and waited for you to come back."

Hephaestus pulled off the cloak that had served as his blanket and draped it around Hestia's shoulders, averting his gaze. She looked down at the remnants of her gown. Little of it remained. Hestia thought even Aphrodite would think twice about revealing so much flesh. She pulled the cloak tightly around her, blushing. She lifted her chin and met Hephaestus's gaze.

"I was with my consort." Hestia said no more, daring him with her silence to ask the obvious question.

The God of the Forge regarded her steadily but didn't speak. A slight grin tugged at the corners of his mouth.

Hestia softened her tone. "You didn't need to wait for me, but it's sweet that you did."

"Yeah, that's us. Sweet," Dionysus grouched as he got stiffly to his feet. "What consort did you find among the boulders and scrub grass?"

"The one who completes me," Hestia said, and smiled at their bewildered expressions. "I need to see about the morning meal. Thank you, both. You're the best friends a goddess could have." She hugged them and left them standing with more questions than answers.

Hestia never told anyone who she spent her one night with. For all accounts, she remained a maiden and minded Zeus's court. No one knew that night after night, the shadow of darkness joined her, caressing, cuddling, and caring for her, the invisible goddess, the one who cared for everyone else.

ABOUT A.C. DAWN

A.C. Dawn is an active and enthusiastic author and reader of short stories, novellas, and novels. She enjoys bringing her characters to life and strives to stir the imagination of her readers. She believes the best writing touches the reader in ways they hadn't expected and will never forget!

So, that's the official bio...
Really, I'm a lover of chocolate, a strong jaw line with a 5 o'clock shadow, and romances that make your heart pound and your middle get all squishy. I love quiet country living on my north Georgia farm with my family and fur babies of all shapes and sizes. I think the scariest thing in life is how fast my daughter is growing and an empty coffee pot. I can't stand slow drivers in the fast lane and wimpy handshakes. I have endless stories rumbling around among the rocks in my head. I can't wait to share them with you!
Want to keep up with me? Follow me here
https://www.facebook.com/A-C-Dawn-
231775085179968o3
https://www.amazon.com/~/e/B08711JGB4

ALSO BY A.C. DAWN

A Stranger's Kiss in Stranded: A Boys Behaving Badly Anthology

Crossing the Line in First Response: A Boys Behaving Anthology

Beyond the Mists in The Once and Future Kingdom Anthology

The Knife's Edge in Samhain Secrets 2 Anthology

The Lady of Sherwood in Ravenous Fables Anthology